"Be Primary School

Wicked Day!

Rob Childs

Illustrated by Michael Reid

CORGI PUPS

WICKED DAY!
A CORGI PUPS BOOK : 9780552547918

First publication in Great Britain

PRINTING HISTORY
Corgi Pups edition published 2002

7 9 10 8 6

Set in 18/25 pt Bembo MT Schoolbook by
Falcon Oast Graphic Art Ltd

Corgi Pups Books are published by Random House Children's Books,
61–63 Uxbridge Road, London W5 5SA,
a division of The Random House Group Ltd.

Addresses for Random House Group Ltd companies outside the UK
can be found at: www.randomhouse.co.uk
The Random House Group Ltd Reg. No. 954009.

Printed and bound in Great Britain by
Cox & Wyman Ltd, Reading, Berkshire.

The Random House Group Limited supports The Forest Stewardship
Council (FSC), the leading international forest certification organisation.
All our titles that are printed on Greenpeace approved FSC certified paper
carry the FSC logo. Our paper procurement policy can be found at:
www.rbooks.co.uk/environment.

Mixed Sources
Product group from well-managed
forests and other controlled sources
www.fsc.org Cert no. TT-COC-2139
© 1996 Forest Stewardship Council
FSC

www.kidsatrandomhouse.co.uk

Contents

Series Reading Consultant: Prue Goodwin,
Lecturer in Literacy and Children's Books,
University of Reading

Wicked Day!

Chapter One
Monday Assembly

"I wonder how many of our *Little Stars* here can tell us why Wednesday this week will be such a special day?"

A forest of hands sprouted towards the hall ceiling.

"Oh, that's splendid!" beamed Miss Humphreys, the head-teacher of Little Fairfield Primary School. "Let me ask . . . um . . ."

Arms strained even higher and straighter to try and catch her attention. She pointed to a boy in Mrs Davison's Year 4 class.

Lee jumped up, accidentally treading on the fingers of the girl next to him, who yelped in pain.

"It's my birthday, Miss!" he announced.

There was a loud burst of
laughter, especially from the
older juniors at the back of the
hall.

"Well, I'm sure that will make
it even more of a special day for

you, Lee," said Miss Humphreys.

"I'm goin' to his party, Miss."

The interruption came from Lee's best friend.

"Never mind that, Bradley," she sighed. "Just tell us what we shall *all* be doing on Wednesday."

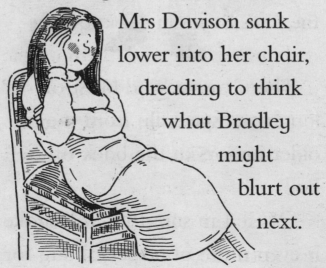

Mrs Davison sank lower into her chair, dreading to think what Bradley might blurt out next.

". . . er . . ." he dithered,
". . . er . . . singin' *Happy
Birthday*, Miss?"

Miss Humphreys
darted a glance over
her spectacles towards
the red-faced teacher.

"Well, let's see whether *any* of
the *Little Angels* in 4D know the
real answer," she said. "Perhaps the
girls do. Shannon, you tell us, please."

Mrs Davison groaned under
her breath. She had just received
a note from Shannon's mum
and guessed what the girl was
going to say.

"I've got the morning off school, Miss, to go to the dentist's."

Miss Humphreys gave up and allowed the children from all the other classes to shout out the answer.

"Altogether now – it's . . ."

"SPORTS DAY!"

As the children trooped out of assembly, Mrs Davison stood by the door, feeling very cross.

"*Little Angels!*" she snorted. "That won't exactly be the name I'll use when I get them back to the classroom."

The caretaker was next to her, leaning on his broom.

"*Little Devils*, more like!" grunted Mr Smith. "Always causing trouble, your lot are. Worst class in the whole school."

Mrs Davison felt that was being a bit harsh.

"I wouldn't go as far as that," she replied, sticking up for them. "Sports-wise, at least, they might even be the best."

"Huh! Roll on Thursday, that's what I say," he muttered.

Chapter Two

Monday Afternoon

"Wicked!" cried Lee as 4D spilled onto the school field for Games. "Look! Roll-On's playing in the sandpit!"

"It's not a sandpit, stupid," sneered Jagdish. "It's a long jump pit."

"Bet he's not playin' either," said Bradley sheepishly. " 'Fraid Dylan did his stuff in there yesterday before I could stop him."

"Did his stuff?" Lee repeated.

"Yeah, y'know what I mean."

Jagdish was disgusted. "Who *is* this Dylan?" he demanded. "Sounds like he needs locking up."

Bradley ran off to the P.E. shed without answering.

"Dylan's his dog," Lee explained before going to help take out some of the equipment from the shed.

The field was soon littered
with skipping ropes, sacks,
hurdles, cones and measuring
tapes for all the children to use.

The long jump pit, however,
remained out of action. Dylan
hadn't been the only four-
legged visitor over the weekend.

"Not a very nice job for you, Roland," said Mrs Davison.

"Dunno what causes me more work," moaned the care-taker, digging his shovel into the sand. "Kids or dogs."

"They shouldn't be allowed to come on here."

"Dead right," he agreed. "Make my life a lot easier, not having all these kids around."

"I meant the dogs," the teacher said as a squabble broke out nearby on the obstacle course. "Mind you, sometimes I think you could be right . . ."

Mrs Davison strode across to the track. "Stop that, you two," she ordered. "Shannon, put Anita down this instant. You're supposed to be giving her a piggy-back, not holding her upside-down like that."

"Sorry, Miss," said Shannon, letting her whimpering partner slide onto the ground in a crumpled heap. "It's just that she called me Fatso."

The teacher sighed. "Well, if she calls you names again, tell her she'll have to carry *you* instead!"

"Roll on home time!" muttered Mr Smith. "That's what I say."

All the children in the school were split up into four different colour teams for Sports Day – Blues, Greens, Reds and Yellows.

Mrs Davison wanted to give 4D's fastest runners in each team another chance to practise the relay. Before the end of the session, the teacher gathered the squads together to work on their change-overs.

"Better to be safe than sorry,"
she advised after a few mishaps.
"It's no good trying to pass the
baton too quickly and risk
dropping it. Too much time is
wasted, having to stop and pick
it up."

When they staged a full
rehearsal for the race, Anita was
leading the way for the Blues.
She sprinted towards Jagdish
and the final change-over, but
he could see that the girl in the
next lane was closing rapidly
on her.

"C'mon, stupid, run!" he
shrieked, thrusting out his right
hand for the baton. "Reds are
catching up!"

Anita stretched her arm
towards the impatient Jagdish.
He snatched at the baton,
fumbled it – and down it went.

Furious, he didn't even bother
to finish the race. He kicked the
baton away in a flash of temper.
"That would be no points at
all for Blues, if it happens again

on Wednesday," Mrs Davison warned him. "And every single point can be vital in the end. Just remember that."

Chapter Three
Tuesday Lunchtime

"Why have you dropped out of the relay, Jag?" Shannon demanded. "It scores double points."

"Couldn't care less," Jagdish retorted.

"Well you should. It might help us Blues win the cup."

She glanced up at the trophy cabinet above the sports notice-board in the corridor. The Athletics Cup still had green ribbons around its handles to show the winning colours from last year's Sports Day.

"What's it to you, anyway?" Jagdish sneered. "You sounded more interested in going to the dentist's in the morning."

Shannon flushed. She was fed up with people still teasing her over that. "No I'm not. I just didn't know what Humpty-Dumpty was going on about."

"Which events you doing tomorrow, Shannon?" put in Lee, who was in the Yellows team.

"Throwing the rounders ball," she said. "Then the long jump and also the obstacle course with Anita."

Jagdish smirked. "You two spend more time arguing than practising."

Shannon felt like hitting him.

"At least we're trying – which is more than can be said for you. Even Connor's taking part with his leg in plaster."

"What's he doing – the three-legged race on his crutches?"

Shannon reacted to the jibe by pushing Jagdish in the chest –

hard enough to make him lose his
balance and go sprawling across
the floor.

He scrambled to his feet,
clenching his fists, but then
turned angrily away and
stormed off.

Lee grinned at Shannon. "Jag didn't really drop out, y'know," he said. "Davey's banned him."

Shannon was shocked. "Why's she done that?"

" 'Cos after Jag got told off by her in Games, he went and kicked one of Callum's crutches away out of spite."

"Didn't know anything about that," she admitted. "I was busy at the pit. Soon as old Roll-On finished there, me and Brad had it all to ourselves."

Bradley was back at the long jump pit after school, surprised to find that he didn't only have Dylan for company.

"What you doin' here, Jag?"

"Not much. Just messing around," Jagdish replied vaguely, avoiding eye contact. He stared instead at the small black dog which was snuffling along the hedge nearby. "Your stupid hound's even scruffier than you. What's it up to now?"

Bradley ignored the taunt. "Dunno," he said with a shrug.
"Probably just sniffin' after rabbits or summat."

"Can't you keep that mutt under control?"

"Course I can," he said and called out to prove it. "Here, boy!"

Bradley should have known better. Dylan glanced up and then lurched away in the opposite direction.

"Huh! One word from you and it does just what it likes," sneered Jagdish, climbing over the wooden fence. "I'm off home."

Bradley wasn't the only one still left on the school premises. While he had a few practice jumps, Mrs Davison was busy at her desk, trying to catch up on some marking.

Yawning, the teacher decided to take a break. She was just on her way to the staffroom to make herself a drink when the caretaker stopped her in the corridor.

"Have *you* got the cup?" Mr Smith demanded.

"My coffee cup?" she said, without thinking.

"The Athletics Cup, of course!" he exclaimed, jabbing a finger up towards the empty space in the cabinet. "It's gone! Wouldn't be surprised if one of your lot's gone and hid it somewhere."

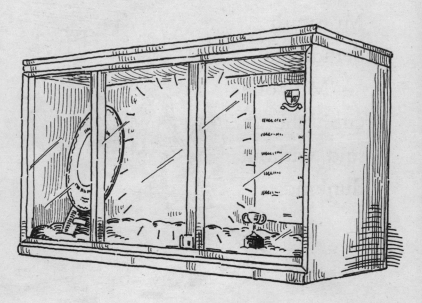

"I'm sure none of them would do such a terrible thing."

"Huh! I'd bet my pension on it," he muttered. "Little monsters!"

Chapter Four
Sports Day

The school field was crowded
with children and parents at the
start of the afternoon – but
there was still no sign of the
missing cup.

The younger juniors were in action first, with Mrs Davison on duty at the pit to measure all the jumps. She had no idea of

how well her pupils were doing elsewhere until somebody came to tell her.

"Shannon won the rounders
ball event, Miss."

"Callum threw the cricket
ball right over the fence, Miss."

"Anita tripped and finished last in the sack race, Miss."

"Lee was winning the obstacle race, Miss, till Dylan got in his way."

Mrs Davison found this last piece of news rather puzzling.

"I don't know anyone called Dylan," she said. "Which class is he in?"

"Nobody's, Miss. Dylan is Bradley's dog," Callum chuckled. "As Lee crawled under the netting, Dylan ran up and started licking him."

Mrs Davison was at least able to enjoy the efforts of some of her own class in the pit.

Several gained maximum points with the length of their jump, but Bradley was unlucky.

"Super jump, Bradley," she praised him, handing over a card to take to the scorers' table where his points would be added to the Yellows total. "It was a pity you fell back onto your bottom after you landed."

The boy didn't seem to mind too much. "Can I go and sit with Mam now, Miss?" he asked. "I've done all my events."

"Yes, of course," she said. "But make sure that dog of yours stays on the lead. It sounds like he's already caused enough trouble for one day."

They say, however, that every dog has its day – and this one most definitely belonged to Dylan.

While the older juniors were going through their paces, it

was also time for a novelty
event on the track — the staff
egg and spoon race.

"C'mon, Miss!" shouted Lee
as the race began. "You can
win this."

"Davey's leading!" cried
Shannon. "Oh no! She's dropped
the egg."

As Mrs Davison tried to
scoop up her wooden egg off
the grass, Mr Smith galloped

past her. The children had never
seen the bow-legged caretaker
move so fast.

It looked like nobody could
stop him winning. The other
teachers kept dropping their eggs,

too, and Miss Humphreys was only waddling along at the back in last place.

With all the cheering, Bradley failed to notice Jagdish sneak up behind him. Suddenly, Dylan's lead was snatched out of his hand and the dog broke free. Dylan scampered onto the track, barking in excitement – straight into the path of the caretaker.

Mr Smith had no chance of avoiding the furry invader. Man and dog collided and crashed to the ground while the spoon flew up into the air.

Dylan was quickly back onto his feet, shaken but unhurt, and picked something up in his mouth out of the grass.

"He's got the spoon!" exclaimed Bradley as the dog ran off. "And look – the egg's still on it!"

"It must be stuck on!" cried Lee. "Roll-On was cheating!"

Dylan crossed the finishing
line just ahead of a giggling
Mrs Davison – his lead, his
young master and all the rest of
the teachers trailing in his wake.

Bradley managed to recapture
Dylan near the hedge.

A glint of silver in the ditch
caught his eye, which he
thought at first must be the
spoon. But there – lying on its
side in the undergrowth – was
the missing cup!

"Leave it!"

The command came not from Bradley, but from a voice behind him. He whirled round to see Jagdish charging towards them.

"How d'yer know what's here, Jag?"

 "Because I put it there, stupid," he admitted. "I was so mad at being banned, I whipped the cup out the cabinet and dumped it."

Bradley bent to fuss his dog. "Dylan's gonna be a big hero now after all the fuss he's caused."

"You're not gonna blab on me, are you?"

Bradley thought for a moment. "No, guess not," he said. "So long as you tell Davey it was you who let Dylan loose."

Bradley grabbed the cup and trotted towards the scorers, Dylan pulling him along on the lead.

"Well done!" cried Miss Humphreys when Bradley plonked the trophy on the table beside her. "What a little treasure you are!"

"Dylan found it, Miss. He deserves all the praise."

The headteacher wasn't quite so sure about that. "Ah, yes, what a little . . ." she began, stumbling for quite the right word to describe the skinny mongrel with grass cuttings stuck in its tangled coat. ". . . um . . . little rascal!"

"It's a dog's life!" muttered Mr Smith, taking the cup into school to polish it up in time for the presentation ceremony. "Roll on summer – that's what I say . . ."

After everyone had finished their events, the Yellows were declared the overall winners – by just a single point. And 4D had

scored more points than any
other class in the school!

Bradley was chosen to receive
the trophy with his Year 6 Yellow
team captain and they held it up
in the air together for all the
clicking cameras.

Dylan crept into the picture,
too, peeking out between them
with a cheeky, lop-sided grin.

Lee's birthday party after
school was a great success. Dylan
was the guest of honour until he
disgraced himself again. He
lapped up a neglected bowl of
trifle and was then sick under the
table.

Lee tied a yellow ribbon
around his birthday cake in
celebration of the team's victory.
"What a wicked day!" he
cried. "Champions!"

THE END

If you enjoyed this sporting tale,
look out for the next Sports
Special by Rob Childs:

WICKED CATCH!
(rounders)

If you like football, you might like
to read about the young footballers
of Great Catesby Primary School in
four smashing tales by Rob Childs,
published by Corgi Pups Books:

GREAT GOAL!
GREAT HIT!
GREAT SAVE!
GREAT SHOT!